for Laura

First published in the U.S.A. 1987
by E. P. Dutton,
2 Park Avenue, New York, N.Y. 10016,
a division of NAL Penguin Inc.

Produced by Mathew Price Ltd

Printed in Hong Kong
First American Edition
ISBN: 0-525-44354-1   OBE
10 9 8 7 6 5 4 3 2 1

Visitors for Edward

written by Michaela Morgan
illustrated by Sue Porter

E. P. Dutton   New York

All night long,

Edward dreamt about his visitors until…

Edward could not have imagined
nicer visitors.

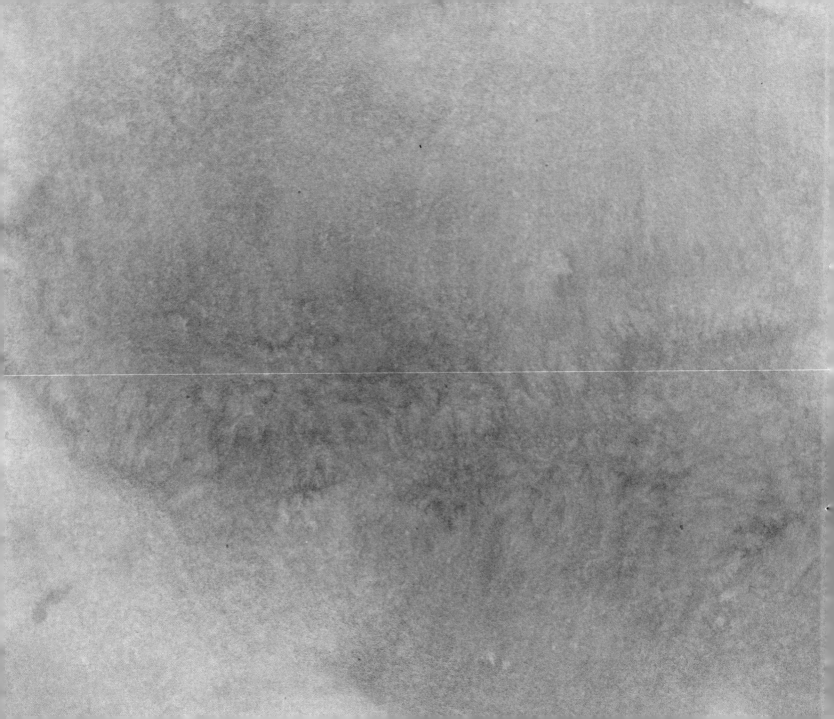